#2

THE DARIO QUINCY ACADEMY OF DANCE

Stolen
LUCK

#2

THE DARIO QUINCY ACADEMY OF DANCE

Stolen LUCK

BY MEGAN ATWOOD

MINNEAPOLIS

Darby Creek
A division of Lerner Publishing Group, Inc.
241 First Avenue North
Minneapolis, MN 55401 U.S.A.

Website address: www.lernerbooks.com

Cover and interior photographs © Marco Costa/Dreamstime.com (main);
© iStockphoto.com/Selahattin BAYRAM (paper background).

Main body text set in Janson Text LT Std 12/17.5.
Typeface provided by Linotype AG.

Library of Congress Cataloging-in-Publication Data

Atwood, Megan.
    Stolen luck / by Megan Atwood.
        pages   cm. — (The Dario Quincy Academy of Dance ; #2)
    ISBN 978–1–4677–0931–6 (lib. bdg. : alk. paper)
    ISBN 978–1–4677–1628–4 (eBook)
    [1. Dance—Fiction. 2. Haunted places—Fiction. 3. Supernatural—
Fiction.] I. Title.
PZ7.A8952St 2013
[Fic]—dc23   2012048710

Manufactured in the United States of America
1 – BP – 7/15/13

To my parents, for their constant support.
And to Patrick, who literally held me up when I
fell down. My love and gratitude to you.

Chapter 1

"No, Kayley! Your turnout is simply poor! You're being lazy—I know you can do a proper turnout! And lift your leg in the arabesque. It droops every time!"

Madame Puant slammed the butt of her cane on the floor and glared at Kayley. Then Madame waved her hand impatiently at Patrick, the pianist, until he stopped playing. Except for the sound of heavy breathing in the room, no one made a peep.

Kayley could feel her face growing hot. Hotter, anyway. She and the others were already an hour and a half into the class, and Kayley was tired. And maybe she *had been* drooping a little—but she didn't think it was fair that Madame called her lazy.

She grumbled under her breath, "Lazy, my butt," then took a peek at her friends. Ophelia looked irritated, like always, probably because she had had to stop dancing. Sophie and Emma were exchanging looks because they couldn't do *anything* without each another, even have a thought. Madeleine stared at Kayley with sympathy.

Madame said, "What was that, Kayley?"

She replied sweetly, "Sorry, Madame."

Madame harrumphed. "You've been sorry all class. That's the second time I've had to interrupt everything for you. Take a break and gain your breath and we'll work on the stepsisters. Sophie, Emma."

Madame nodded to Patrick, who played a hint of what the orchestra would sound like when the class actually put on the show.

Kayley walked to the side of the room, avoiding the gazes of her classmates. She slumped down next to her bag and threw her legs in a wide split, pretending to stretch down to the floor so she wouldn't have to look at anyone. Her legs were sore. Maybe over fall break she should have practiced more often.

Coming back to the school after seeing her family in Connecticut had been more than a little hard. As the youngest sibling out of five, Kayley loved being home with her big family. All four of her brothers were superstars in some way, of course. Her oldest brother was literally a brain surgeon in Boston. The next oldest one was a lawyer in New York, and the next one was a professional tennis player. The brother closest to her, still in college, was planning to be a psychologist *and* a psychiatrist. He would, too, because he was by far the smartest person in her already smart family.

And then there was Kayley.

Kayley loved to dance. She really did. It was

just that everyone expected so much of her all the time. Even over fall break, in the middle of a laughing episode at dinner, Kayley's dad pounced.

"So, are you up for any leads this year, Kay?"

She hated it when he called her Kay.

"Daaaad. I told you, I got fairy godmother in *Cinderella*." She took a big bite of her mom's lasagna and added, "It's a solo part. Everyone loves that part."

Her dad frowned at her. "But no leads. Maybe you should practice more. We could set you up—"

She shook her head impatiently. "I want to have an actual break during my break!"

Kayley could feel the disappointment wafting off of him.

"OK, honey," he winked. "Anyway, we can't wait to see you dance whatever part you dance." And then he ignored her once again and started talking to Brian, her oldest brother, about his possible upcoming job as chief of neurosurgery. The pride in his face could've made anyone teary.

Kayley stared down at her lasagna and put her fork down. Suddenly, she wasn't hungry.

And now, a week later, Kayley couldn't seem to even dance the fairy godmother role, let alone a lead part.

She leaned down and touched her forehead to the ground, feeling the pounding of pointe shoes as Emma and Sophie danced. She could feel it when Ophelia jumped in. People always thought ballet dancers were delicate, but if they could hear the floor when the dancers jumped . . .

She felt someone sit down beside her but refused to look up. A voice whispered in her ear, "Everyone has bad days."

Kayley sat up and smiled at Madeleine. She really was the nicest person. Also an incredible dancer, but because Madeleine was new to the academy, she was only in the corps this performance. It was only a matter of time, though, until Madeleine started to land lead roles. Ophelia had some competition.

And Madeleine's talent was only part of it, Kayley thought. Yes, Madeleine had musicality, and yes, she had a grace that couldn't be taught, no matter who was doing the teaching. But she also came to class early every day and practiced. Kayley couldn't even think about that. She already felt it was torture to be up at six. And she was almost always late.

She shrugged at Madeleine. "It's all right. Madame needs someone to yell at. I guess I'm the lucky one today."

And the last few days, she thought.

Madame clapped her hands, which meant it was the end of class and time for reverence—the period when the ballet dancers thanked their teacher through dance and paid respect. Kayley couldn't think of anything she'd like to do less. She got up, went through the motions, and finished just slightly before everyone else. She was already at her bag by the time everyone else finished the movements. When she looked up, she could see Madame's angry eyes flicker over her and then look away. Kayley flinched. She didn't like that look.

She got out a gummy worm from her bag—so what if it was only nine in the morning?—and started to chew on it. This was definitely not her day. She shrugged. The afternoon practice would just have to be better.

Chapter 2

But afternoon practice was not better. Not by an inch.

Kayley just couldn't seem to catch up. Her counting was off, and she literally tripped over her own feet during two of the moves.

With a look of disgust, Madame waved for her to go sit down. Kayley, secretly relieved and trying to hide her heavy breathing, slunk happily to the floor.

And then her world collapsed.

"Madeleine, have you been watching the godmother scenes?"

Madeleine stole a quick glance at Kayley, then nodded her head.

"Well, do you think you could dance them?"

Kayley stared at Madame. Was she doing what Kayley thought she was doing? Suddenly, more than the tough dance routine was causing sweat to trickle down Kayley's spine.

Madeleine looked at her guiltily and nodded to Madame.

"Let's try them. Patrick, from the top of the fairy godmother scene."

The pianist began the music that started the scene.

And Kayley sat horrified as she watched Madeleine take her place.

The worst thing about the whole affair was that Madeleine *should* have been taking her place. She was wonderful.

Kayley watched as Madeleine performed every move flawlessly. Two fouettés, an arabesque that lasted forever, bourrées ... Kayley couldn't watch anymore.

Madeleine had danced Kayley's part perfectly. And with a sinking feeling, Kayley realized what that meant.

When Madeleine was finished, the whole class clapped, and Kayley's face burned. She felt tears behind her eyes, and she could feel people stealing glances at her. Madeleine looked down at the floor and frowned. Kayley knew she felt bad. But she also knew Madeleine just couldn't help being a good dancer.

Madame said curtly, "OK, Madeleine, you dance the fairy godmother. Kayley, you try corps. Patrick, let's go from the top of Cinderella's entrance. Ophelia, take your place."

And with that, Kayley's dream was crushed.

Madeleine walked toward her with a worried expression on her face. The rest of the class looked on.

Kayley didn't cry. With four brothers, she had grown up pretty tough. At least that's what she told herself. And she certainly didn't cry in public. But she felt the tears welling up and knew they would spill soon. The minute Madeleine said a word to her, Kayley was sure she'd lose it.

So she did something she'd never done before: she ran out of ballet class.

She grabbed her bag and darted around the front of the room, behind a flabbergasted Madame and in front of the whole class. But she didn't care. The situation was more than humiliating, and she needed to get out before the tears spilled.

She ran all the way to her room, down the sinister hallway with flickering candle lights and red carpet, and made it to her door as the first sob came. She unlocked the door quickly, then fell on her bed, the sobs coming harder and faster.

What would she tell her dad? Her brothers? How could this have happened?

She sat up and threw her bag against the wall, then buried her face in her pillow and screamed.

She had been a dancer—a soloist—for as long as she could remember. She had always been the best in the class until she came to Dario Quincy Academy. But she didn't mind not being the best once she came here because the dancing was so fun and amazing, and the other dancers pushed her to be better. And she'd worked hard, at least for a couple of years, to get to be a soloist. And in one fell swoop, she had been demoted back to the corps.

With the fourteen-year-olds and the ones that everyone knew would never get a professional ballet job.

She was just another corps dancer.

The sobs turned into anger. Who did Madame think she was, to treat her this way? What did Madame know anyway? Kayley deserved the part of the fairy godmother—it was hers!

Just then, her door opened and Ophelia, Sophie, Emma, and—way in the back— Madeleine stood in the hall, looks of pity on their faces. Even Ophelia, who had the empathy of a pigeon, looked sympathetic.

Kayley wiped her cheeks and said, "I want to be alone."

Ophelia walked in anyway and threw a bag of Sour Patch Kids on her bed, then flopped onto Kayley's desk chair. Sophie and Emma followed and sat down on her floor. Finally, Madeleine came in and leaned awkwardly on her dresser, her eyes looking everywhere but at Kayley.

Kayley sighed. Friends don't listen when you want to be alone.

Ophelia pointed to the package of Sour Patch Kids. "We thought you might want those."

Despite herself, Kayley was touched. Ophelia was always taking candy out of her hand and throwing it away. So she knew her friends understood, in some way, what she was going through. But Kayley shook her head anyway.

"Not hungry."

She could feel Sophie and Emma looking at each other and could imagine what they were thinking. That Kayley never turned down sweets. And Kayley never did. Except, apparently, when she was failing at life.

She picked at her bedspread.

Madeleine cleared her throat and said, "Kayley..." Suddenly her eyes were full of tears. "I'm so sorry. I don't know what to do. If you want me not to dance it..."

Kayley was truly touched. No ballet dancer in the history of the world would turn down a better part if she were able to do it. So as much as Kayley wanted to, she told herself that she wouldn't deny Madeleine the part.

She shook her head and sighed. "No, Madame wants you to do it." Kayley smiled. "And it's not your fault. So don't feel sorry about it." She meant it too. Madeleine was too nice to be mad at.

And, anyway, Kayley knew where to lay the blame: Madame Puant. Suddenly, resolve took the place of her sadness. She was not going to lie down and take this.

She smiled bigger at Madeleine. "But don't think I won't fight for the role."

Madeleine's smile was warm and big too. A collective sigh of relief filled the room.

Opening the package, she dumped out a Sour Patch Kid and popped it in her mouth. She felt good again. Powerful. She would make this right.

"Tomorrow I'm going to have a little talk with Madame and set her straight."

She caught a tiny frown line between Ophelia's eyes and saw a look pass between Ophelia and Madeleine. Madeleine looked relieved, but Ophelia looked dubious.

A tickle of unease danced up Kayley's spine. Ophelia shared looks with her, not Madeleine. Dumping out more candy, Kayley put the thought out of her mind and began to strategize for her talk with Madame.

Chapter 3

"Even you have to admit, your work has been sloppy as of late," Madame said, as she shuffled papers that covered her huge, ornately carved desk.

Kayley squirmed in her chair. There was something about Madame that made her feel small, even though Kayley was probably two inches taller. Madame could look down her nose at you from any height.

Kayley swallowed. All the fire she'd felt the

night before seemed to have gone up in smoke. She nodded shakily. Then she added, "Lately. But you know I'm not like that all the time."

Madame stopped shuffling papers. Kayley thought she seemed burdened with the world. But what she realized she saw was Madame looking sad. Her eyes were downcast, and her mouth was pressed and turned down. Madame was sad to have to do this. Kayley shifted in her seat.

Madame leaned forward and said softly, "Not all the time. But for all of the semester to date. And after autumn break, well . . . things have only gone downhill. Your concentration is off; your technique is poor. You're a different dancer than you were just a year ago. I gave you the part of the fairy godmother with the hopes that you'd find yourself again. But you haven't."

Kayley's eyes filled with tears. She cursed herself and her stupid tear ducts. This talk was not going quite how she planned. She would *not* cry in front of Madame. With a huge effort, she swallowed down the lump of emotion in her throat.

"Madame ... I know things have been a little sloppy lately. But I *will* get better and back to myself. I'm just asking for another chance."

Madame shook her head and gave her the sad look again. "Kayley, do you think professional ballet companies give dancers another chance? This school is supposed to prepare you for your career as a dancer. Your *professional* career. Only the best get into this academy, and we have a 95 percent placement rate. And that's saying something when ballet is on the decline.

"There's nothing to be ashamed of, being in the corps. Nothing. That's a huge accomplishment in and of itself. We'll place you, no doubt. So why don't you just enjoy your dancing now? You seem to be at a place where your performance has taken second fiddle to ... well, to something, and that's fine. You have that luxury because of natural talent. So enjoy yourself."

A tear spilled over Kayley's cheek. How could she explain to Madame that second best was never good enough? That in her family, dancing the corps might as well be a prison term and a life of crime? It was bad enough she didn't have the lead but the corps? Her parents would never be proud of her. Unlike her brothers. She was officially the black sheep of the family. She could never endure them coming to the *Cinderella* production.

Madame got up and walked around the desk, sitting beside Kayley in one of her office's massive leather chairs. In an uncharacteristic motherly move, Madame wiped the tear off Kayley's cheek.

"Kayley," she said softly. "There are only two weeks until the performance. My hands are tied. We need someone who can dance the part."

Kayley sniffled and then stopped fighting it. She let the tears flow.

Madame grabbed a box of Kleenex sitting on her desk. How often did she have to hand out tissues to crying dancers? Kayley wondered. She blew her nose noisily and wiped her eyes.

"I think you are a beautiful dancer, Kayley,

with a lot of potential. But I don't think you have the drive that others here do. And that's OK."

Kayley hiccup-sobbed and grabbed another Kleenex.

Madame went on, "But if you want to convince me otherwise, well, *convince me*! Eat, breathe, *live* ballet. Read books in the library, practice off-hours." She glanced at Kayley's bag. "Eat healthy and nourish your body instead of feeding it junk. Then, perhaps, for the next production, you will have earned your place as a soloist."

Madame stood up decisively and strolled back behind her desk. "But you'll have to really show me. Otherwise, be satisfied with your place in the corps. Many dancers would kill for that, you know."

She winked at Kayley.

Kayley took a deep breath. No way was she going to be content with the corps. No way. She stiffened her spine and grabbed her bag. "OK. I've heard everything you have to say, Madame."

And then Kayley walked out of the office.

Maybe she wouldn't kill someone for a place in the corps or even a lead part but darned if she wouldn't kill herself trying to get back on top if she had to.

Chapter 4

As much as Kayley didn't want to admit it. Madame was right. She wasn't driven. She didn't care as much as the others. And she didn't eat, sleep, and breathe ballet.

But she knew she was talented. Maybe not as talented as Madeleine and Ophelia but definitely more so than Sophie and Emma. Or at least on the same level.

As if she had called the girls up, all four of them came down the hall toward her. She had missed dinner to speak to Madame, and she knew the others were all curious as to what had happened.

She kept walking down the hall and met them halfway. The dark corridor did nothing to dampen her mood. For the first time in days, she felt happy. And determined.

"Hey, guys!" she said as she reached Ophelia, Madeleine, Sophie, and Emma. Ophelia furrowed her eyebrows. Ophelia was one of those girls, Kayley knew, who always looked mad or just plain mean. So when Ophelia actually put on a stern face, her look was plain paralyzing. Normally, Kayley would have laughed at the look, but something had changed in her. She stared back and said, "What."

"What do you mean, what?" Ophelia said. "I was just looking at you. Wondering how it went with Madame."

Ophelia looked at Madeleine and widened her eyes.

A pang of jealousy shot through Kayley. Since when were Ophelia and Madeleine such good friends? Not only was Madeleine taking her part, but evidently she was taking Kayley's friends as well. If Madeleine weren't so nice, Kayley would actually be angry with her. But she couldn't think of her friendships now. She had work to do.

She continued down the hall, the girls following her. Kayley could practically feel their confusion.

Finally, Sophie spoke up: "Well?"

Kayley stopped in front of her room. "Well, what?"

Ophelia let out an exasperated sigh. "You know what! How did it go with Madame?"

Kayley turned the key in her lock. "It was really good."

Emma's eyes widened. "Did Madame give you your part back?"

Madeleine looked relieved. Kayley realized how conflicted she must have felt about taking the role. She truly wasn't upset with Madeleine about it either, but she didn't have time to babysit other people's feelings.

She opened her door and said, "Nope," then stepped inside, leaving the four girls standing outside in the hall.

Madeleine reached out with another bag of candy. "We thought you might like one of these. Talking to Madame is always hard."

Kayley smiled at the girls. "Thanks, but no thanks. You guys are great. But I need to do some work. I'll see you tomorrow morning at class."

With that, she shut the door.

***

It was one in the morning, and Kayley had been in the library for hours, paging through books on ballet technique. She'd exhausted herself in her room browsing the Internet and watching YouTube. For variety, she'd decided to check out the library—a place she hadn't even stepped in since she started coming to the academy two years ago. She'd managed to carve a space out in the way, way back corner of the dusty shelves so she could try out any new moves she discovered.

She wondered if anyone else had ever gone back to the place where she had camped out—a forgotten-looking corner at the end of a labyrinth of corridors. Cobwebs hung from the dusty old windows, and the books on the shelves looked ancient. The lights in the library had been shut off hours ago, but Kayley had planned ahead and kept her flashlight. She'd broken curfew so many times before that she knew exactly how to prepare lights-out. Sure, she was risking detention—or worse—but she wasn't nervous in the least. She had a feeling that no one would check all the way back where she was. She hadn't even known the place existed.

Even though Kayley wasn't one to get easily spooked, she had to admit this corner of the library was creepy. Cut off from everything else, dark and dusty . . . Every noise threatened to make her jump. And there were a lot of noises. Creaks, groans, sighs. The place sounded like it was talking at her in a dead language. She was officially creeped out.

As she was closing a book on Russian masters and their ballet techniques, she thought she heard footsteps.

Her heart began to beat faster, and blood rushed to her head. She sat still and listened, but the footsteps no longer sounded through the hall.

She shook her head. The dark corner and the echoing sounds were getting to her. Lots of students thought the academy was haunted, but she never believed in that kind of stuff.

She stood up. From three shelves away, a loud *bang* echoed through the room like a shot.

Kayley jumped back, toppling over the chair she was sitting on. She put a hand to her chest, trying to slow her fast-beating heart. She flashed her light around the space and called out in a shaky voice, "Who's there?"

The only reply was the echo of her question.

Her flashlight beam landed on cobwebs, revealing shelves filled with the crumbling old books. A spider crawled along the top of one of the cases.

She shivered. Yep, it was time to get out of there.

Grabbing the books she'd collected, she walked quickly down a row of stacks until she tripped and dropped her flashlight. It rolled away from her, spinning and spinning until it stopped, like a spotlight, on the object that had caused her fall.

Kayley bent down and looked at it—a book. An ancient one, from the looks of it. Turning it over in the light, she scanned the cover: *A History of Dario Quincy Academy of Dance.* She shrugged to herself. It wouldn't hurt to read up on the place.

As she picked the book up, her bag bumped against the bookcase, and from the upper tier of the library, Kayley could swear she heard laughter. She stayed still for a moment to see if it came back, and though no noises did, a feeling of unease crept up her spine.

Why was she listening for voices in an empty library? she asked herself and then ran as fast as she could to her room.

Chapter 5

Despite a promise to herself that she would get a good night's sleep for ballet class after her adventure in the library, Kayley found herself transfixed.

A History of Dario Quincy Academy of Dance was captivating.

After her experience in the creepy corner, Kayley had run back to her room, shadows following her wherever she went. She unlocked her door and stumbled into her room. She landed on her bed, and without putting on pajamas, she opened the old book.

Dust puffed out and Kayley coughed. She dropped the book, startled, and it landed open to a page with a beautifully illustrated picture of pointe shoes, old-fashioned but still gorgeous. Kayley was mesmerized. She picked the book back up and read the caption underneath the illustration: "The dancing shoes of Dorothy Quincy, wife of the founder of Dario Quincy Academy."

Something like recognition flashed through her mind, but she couldn't quite grab onto it. She started reading the section.

The book talked about the founder of the academy and how bad luck seemed to follow him wherever he went. Until he married a ballerina and together they established the academy, as well as a company with her dancing the lead. Evidently, she was a beautiful dancer, which seemed to make up for her husband's bad luck, and she was on her way toward world renown as a prima ballerina.

Dorothy was very superstitious and made

sure to wear the same pointe shoes for every performance, mending them as they needed to be mended and tending to them with great care. And then one day, they were gone. Vanished.

She was heartbroken, but she was a dancer and she had to dance. And so she still performed, on borrowed pointe shoes, in the academy's production of *Giselle*. It was during this performance that an accident took her life. She died before she could become famous.

Legend also had it that the shoes reappeared after Dorothy's death and her husband kept them with him every night until his death. His luck then changed—the academy expanded, his fortune grew, but his heart remained broken. Regardless, the rumor was that the shoes imparted good luck on anyone who had them in their possession.

By the time Kayley closed the book, a vision flashed in her brain. The shoes were at the academy, enclosed in a glass case in the lobby. She'd seen them a million times, read the plaque in front of them over and over without retaining any of it. She could see the inscription in her mind, plain as day: "In loving memory of Dorothy Quincy. May your dancing live on."

Kayley shut the book. She could sure use some luck like that at this point. She looked at the clock and yawned. Three in the morning already, and class started in three hours. She sighed. Looked like it would be another humiliating class.

**

After class, a sweaty Kayley left early to avoid talking to her friends. She'd been right—it *had* been an awful class. Kayley was just too tired to give it her all, and it showed in the corps. She kept yawning through the practice, and more than once she felt the harsh eyes of Madame staring at her. She walked out, discouraged.

To avoid breakfast and other people, Kayley walked downstairs and headed in the opposite direction of the dining hall. She would just wander until the meal was over and then head to regular classes. She didn't even feel like taking a shower. She stepped out into the lobby of the building and saw the glass case right away. She'd always taken that case for granted. But there they were.

The shoes.

She hurried over to the case and stared at them.

If only she could have them, just for a little while, just until her dancing returned to the level it had been at.

She could make her dad proud. And Madame.

Kayley looked all around the glass case to see if she could open it somehow, just to touch the shoes one time. A lock sat at the back of the display.

Kayley sighed in frustration. Of course the case was locked. Did she think she could just open the case and touch an antique pair of shoes?

She shook her head, annoyed with herself. What was she thinking, anyway? That these shoes could really make someone a better dancer? It was a silly thought for a silly girl. She turned around and ran smack into Bert, the maintenance man, making the keys on his belt jingle.

He scowled down at her. "Watch where you're going, missy."

She stepped back, and he grabbed a bottle of cleaner and started wiping the glass case.

"Now don't you go smudging this case, Ms. Thing. I have to wipe this down every day, and I'll be able to tell."

Kayley laughed. "I was just *looking* at them."

He scowled at her, and she backed away, but not before she took note of his large key ring.

She would bet her entire ballet career that the key to that case was on that ring. And the strange feeling of need came over Kayley. She wanted those shoes. More than anything else in the world.

She stood straighter. What would it hurt to test the legend?

Chapter 6

On her way back to her room, Kayley ran into Madeleine and Ophelia. They were whispering to each other and giggling. Kayley seethed with jealousy. Madeleine *was* taking everything away from her. Ophelia was supposed to be *Kayley's* best friend.

She tried to walk past them without saying anything, but Ophelia grabbed her sweater. "Hey. Where are you going?"

"Are you all right?" Madeleine asked,

putting a hand on Kayley's shoulder.

Kayley shrugged it off. "I'm fine. Just not feeling well, that's all."

Ophelia stared hard at her. Kayley knew she wasn't buying it. But Ophelia shrugged and said, "Whatever."

Madeleine said, "Do you want us to walk you to the nurse's office?"

The nurse's office was perfect. Why hadn't she thought of that? It was right near the staircase to the lower floor, where Bert's office was. She would fake sick all day and use the time away from class to try to get the keys.

Kayley shook her head. "Uh, no, I can get there myself. I'm just going to drop off my bag." She looked down at the floor and started to walk away.

"You're acting weird," Ophelia said, but Kayley was walking away too fast to respond. She dismissed the other girls with a wave. She didn't have time for this; she had an illness to fake.

She dropped her bag off in her room, then grabbed a hooded sweatshirt with a pocket in the front. Then she practically sprinted to the nurse's room.

When she got there, she tried her hardest to look sick.

The nurse was cleaning shelves off as Kayley walked in. She held her belly and groaned to get the nurse's attention.

He turned around.

"My stomach hurts."

Nurse John squinted at her. "Well, why don't you lie here. Have you eaten today?"

This was always his first question. Nurse John thought ballet dancers didn't eat enough.

She realized she hadn't. She shook her head.

He frowned and then walked to his desk and pulled out a granola bar. "Well, eat this. Then we'll see how you feel."

Kayley nodded, opened up the wrapper, and ate the bar. Her stomach actually did start to feel better, but she waited for a bit and said, "I don't think that helped." She tried to look as pitiful as she could.

Then she added, "I don't think I can do classes or ballet practice today."

Now the nurse, Kayley knew, was used to ballet dancers trying to fake sick out of regular classes. But never did they try to fake their way out of ballet class. Never. Nurse John immediately nodded and said, "OK. I'll give you a note to give to your teachers. Can you make it to your room all right?"

Kayley nodded and watched as he scribbled something on a piece of paper. She could hardly believe how easy this was: all she had to do was show the note to Madame and her teachers tomorrow, and she'd be excused. She had to hide her smile when the nurse handed her the paper.

She held her stomach and said, "Thank you," and walked slowly out the door.

As she turned the corner, she looked both ways down the hall to make sure no one would see her, then went down the stairs she knew led to the maintenance man's room.

Time to change things around. Time for the shoes.

When Kayley hit the first stair, she almost turned back. She had forgotten how creepy the school could be. There was barely any light in the staircase. Canned laughter traveled to her from a TV far away, coming from the bottom of the stairs. The house creaked and groaned. Shadows played down the stairway, even though it was the middle of the day. She knew there were no windows down in the basement. She wondered how the maintenance man handled it. She could see why he was slightly weird.

She crept down ancient wooden stairs and, after an eternity, got to the end. Light flooded out into the hallway from a room off to her right, the source of the TV laughter. She sidled up to the door, tiptoeing. She crouched down, thinking Bert wouldn't notice a face at the bottom of the door, and moved her head around the corner.

The office was empty.

Papers stood everywhere in uneven stacks, and a prehistoric computer sat blank-screened and unused on the desk. The TV sat on top of a double VCR/DVD player, with some tape going in the VCR. It looked and sounded like old episodes of some old TV show. Who knew? The maintenance man was a sitcom lover. Vintage.

Kayley slipped into the maintenance room as quietly as she could. The first thing she did was step on a pencil. The sound ricocheted off the room.

Kayley ducked, putting her hands up to her mouth. She looked out to the hallway, but no one seemed to be coming.

Looking carefully at the floor in front of her, she tiptoed over to the desk and began opening its metallic drawers. Each one squeaked open. The bottom drawer held a series of files. Kayley noticed an entire folder dedicated to *Giselle*, but she didn't have time to look at it. She was searching for a key. Surely Bert had duplicates?

She stepped back and scanned the room. Nothing.

She needed those shoes! She kicked her heel back against the wall, not caring whether or not someone heard her. Something banged against her calf, and she turned around.

A tiny door in the wall hung open, about an inch up from the wood trim at bottom. She never would have seen the door's outline unless she'd been looking for it. Crouching down,

Kayley looked inside. An old-fashioned key hung on a hook.

A key that looked like a perfect fit for the display case upstairs.

Kayley reached out slowly and picked the key up, holding it in her hands. Here was the key to her future. The key to dancing the part she was supposed to dance. To being the dancer she wanted to be. She closed the little door and stood up. And then she heard it again. The laughter. This time she was sure.

Shoving the key in her pocket, she sprinted upstairs to her room, making enough noise to wake the dead.

Chapter 7

At midnight, Kayley sat on her bed, chewing on her fingernails, her knees shaking. She'd been going over the same thoughts constantly since she took the key.

Should she, or shouldn't she?

Kayley hadn't even gone to dinner. She had just lain on her bed, one arm thrown across her eyes and the other tapping its fingers on the bedspread.

Taking the shoes would be wrong. No doubt

about it. She would get into *major* trouble if someone found out. She might even get kicked out of the academy and then she wouldn't be able to get into another one and then she'd never get a position in a company . . . Her parents would be so ashamed. Not to mention, her own moral compass pointed to no. Stealing was just wrong.

But then . . .

Kayley needed that part back. She was born to play the fairy godmother. She needed to feel that fire in her belly again, the whole-body feeling that came over her when she would get a complicated move right or when she could feel the music run through her. She *needed* it.

And it sure as heck wasn't anywhere to be found at the moment.

Kayley stopped shaking her knees and stood up straight. She'd wasted yet another hour worrying. It was time for action. Even if the shoes *didn't* work as a good luck charm, well . . . she'd know she'd tried everything.

Opening her door quietly, she looked both ways down the hallway. Dark shadows played all around the hall, the electric lights on the wall flickering like candles. The bloodred carpet looked almost black in the shadows. Kayley shivered.

As long as she didn't hear that laugh, she'd be fine. She hoped.

Kayley stepped lightly down the hallway, slowing near the set of big stairs that lead to the lobby. She took a look over the edge of the ornate banister and saw the dark entrance into the lobby area. A red light from the Exit sign on the side of the huge lobby seemed to shine in a beam that led straight to the shoe display. She walked carefully down the wide marble staircase. Her slippers made only the tiniest *shush* as she walked.

After what seemed like a decade, Kayley reached the bottom. For a second, she hesitated, wringing her hands together. She looked down at her feet, set automatically in first position. She smiled a little to herself; Madame would love her turnout right now.

With the thought of Madame propelling her, Kayley moved forward into the dark of the lobby, following the light that led to the shoes.

She stopped in front of the glass case and looked down.

The glow from the Exit sign made the cream color of the shoes a ghostly red. Kayley hesitated again.

Suddenly, the sound of whistling traveled downward from the hallway opposite the stairs.

The maintenance man! Of course, Bert did nightly checks around the building! More than one ballet dancer had been caught during his rovings.

Kayley crept behind a huge leather chair that sat in the lobby. And just in time. The whistling got louder—she could hear the clomping of his boots as he walked through the lobby.

The maintenance man made his way past the case and toward Kayley. She knew she was well hidden, but her heart felt like it would crawl out of her chest anyway.

And then it happened. Kayley's leg started to cramp up. She knew she needed to switch positions. She shifted ever so slightly, and the key fell out of her hoodie pocket, clinking on the marble ground.

The whistling stopped immediately.

"Who's there?"

The maintenance man's voice echoed through the lobby. Kayley thought for sure she'd pass out.

His boots came trudging toward Kayley's hiding spot, so she picked up the key and shifted her weight until she was completely hidden behind the chair.

And then her leg cramped again. She clamped her lips down hard and stayed in position, ignoring the pain. Bert grumbled, "If it's any kids, you all are in trouble."

But Kayley thought she heard some fear in his voice. What did *he* have to be afraid of?

After a torturous few minutes, Bert walked away. Kayley heard him say under his breath, "You won't beat me yet, Quincy house. I'm not afraid of you."

She could tell from the quiver in his voice that he was most definitely afraid.

When she heard his boots make it all the way down the hallway, she stood up and shook out her leg. It was time to get out of the lobby before someone else decided to come in and talk to themselves.

Kayley ran to the box and slid in the key. Sure enough, it fit. She opened the case. A rush of musty smell enveloped her nose, but she reached in and picked up the shoes, moving slowly and gently to make sure she didn't damage them.

They were tiny and fragile. And they were beautiful.

Carefully placing one and then the other in the front pocket of her hoodie, she closed the lid and locked it.

A strange calm enveloped her, and she walked slowly back to her room, her only thought the steady, reassuring notion that she would once again be the dancer she wanted to be.

Chapter 8

Kayley got no sleep that night. After staring at the shoes and touching them ever so lightly, she had to figure out a place to put them. Someplace safe, not only from someone finding them but also for the shoes. She was mesmerized by them and didn't want them to get dirty.

Hiding something in your room was problematic. Kayley had seen searches before when things were stolen . . . She couldn't risk being caught. She bounced her knee up and down and racked her brain for the solution.

And then she figured it out. The best hiding place was in plain sight. She had slippers shaped like sushi that were plush and huge. She'd put one shoe in each slipper. The shoes would stay pristine, and if anyone decided to do a search, who would check the sushi slippers?

She swore, as she tucked the hidden shoes away in her closet, that she felt an extra little charge. Maybe today would be a good day for dancing. She glanced up at the clock: five thirty. She might as well go to class now and do a good warm-up. And anyway, she was dying to see if there was any effect.

She quickly changed into her leotard and footless tights and tied her hair up in a bun. With a quick look to the closet, where her new lucky shoes lay, she grabbed her bag and raced out the door. She felt electric.

* * *

Kayley did a few jumping jacks to get her blood pumping once she reached the ballet studio. She didn't realize how tight her body had been. She decided to take her time stretching, enjoying every single movement of the pull. She'd forgotten how nice it was to really concentrate on stretching. She did use to come early to do these stretches; maybe she'd get back in the habit.

At quarter to six, Madeleine walked in and practically jumped in surprise at Kayley.

Even though Kayley knew Madeleine didn't mean to steal everything of Kayley's, a part of her still felt resentful. But with the thought of the shoes in her closet, she also felt a little . . . well, superior to her all of a sudden. Superior and just a little snotty.

"Hey, what are you doing in here?" Madeleine asked.

Kayley smiled sweetly and said, "Ballet."

Madeleine's face turned red. "Of course. I mean . . . I just haven't . . . that's cool. Maybe we can warm-up together."

Kayley smiled again. "You know, I think I've done the stretching. I'm going to practice some turns now."

She took her shoes out of the bag—they seemed so odd now that she'd been looking at the old-fashioned ones—and tied them tight. She flexed her feet. The shoes felt so good, so right. That electric feeling came back. She felt like she could dance up a storm.

She stood up and did a trial pirouette. Just as she spotted, her gaze landed on Ophelia, a scowl on Ophelia's pretty face.

She said to Kayley, "What are you doing in here?"

Kayley got off pointe and said the same thing she said to Madeleine: "Ballet." Then she did three fouettés in a row and ended in a side split on pointe. The electricity practically crackled.

Ophelia gaped at her. Kayley smiled with her face toward the ground. It had to be the shoes.

Madame walked in, as did the rest of the company, and Kayley saw it was already five minutes to six. Madame called them all to attention and class began. Kayley had a good feeling about this.

***

Perfection. That was the word that kept running through her mind. *Perfection.*

She knew the class saw the change in her. She kept getting looks and this time because Madame used her as a *good* example. At the end of class, she approached Madame with her excused-absence note.

Madame stared down at her behind small, leopard-printed reading glasses and said, "Well, whatever rest you got yesterday must have done the trick."

Kayley just smiled. Madame signed the note and said, "If you keep dancing like this, maybe there will be a lead part in our next production."

Kayley's stomach sank. "But, Madame, can't I have the fairy godmother part back? That is, you know, if I keep dancing like I am?"

Madame shook her head. "Kayley, I can't change back now. We're too close to the start of the production, and it's just too strange to go back and forth. I'm sorry, but you'll have to stay in the corps this ballet. The next one, though . . ."

She shot a pointed look toward Kayley, a look that said "this is important," and added, "*If* you keep dancing like this."

Kayley walked angrily over to her bag. What was the point of all of this? She had just danced better than ever before, better than Madeleine. Why couldn't she get her part back? Had she stolen the shoes for nothing? She picked up her bag as Sophie ran into the room.

"Did you hear?" Sophie asked excitedly.

Kayley shook her head.

"Somebody stole the shoes in the case out front!" Sophie said.

Kayley remembered that she needed to look surprised. She put her hands up to her mouth and made a squeak she hoped sounded like shock.

Sophie nodded, "I know! Who would want to steal those shoes?"

Kayley shrugged. "Yeah, that's really weird."

"Honestly, what some people will do for attention here."

Kayley narrowed her eyes. Sophie, busy walking to the back of the class, didn't see it. She picked a shrug from off the floor.

"I forgot this," she said to Kayley and walked toward the door. Turning around, she added.

"Hey, you were awesome in class today! I'm glad to see you're finally trying."

Kayley fumed. Finally trying? Needed attention? She wasn't some little kid throwing a tantrum. And it's not like she hadn't *been* trying. Well, maybe not as hard but still.

She walked out the door, determined to show Sophie what *trying* really meant at their next class.

Chapter 9

The whole school was abuzz about the shoes. Kayley felt a little guilty thrill every time she heard about it. In English class, Mr. Boynton made an announcement:

There would be room searches that night.

Kayley had only a slight trickle of sweat at the thought. She felt she'd hidden the shoes well.

She hoped.

Madeleine tapped her on the shoulder as the English lesson started.

"Hey," she whispered, "that was some awesome dancing."

Kayley turned around and gave her a cold smile. "Thanks."

Madeleine looked so genuine all the time. It was starting to bother Kayley lately.

She didn't know why, but she just felt mean.

"You know, I haven't seen you lugging around that big bag of Sour Patch Kids we got you."

Kayley shrugged. "I'm not twelve anymore," she said and turned around. She could practically feel Madeleine's quizzical look.

Three minutes later, a paper ball landed on her desk. Kayley looked over to Ophelia, a few rows over, who was frantically gesturing to her to open it.

Kayley was annoyed—all of a sudden they wanted to talk to her? Still, with Ophelia's eyes on her, she opened the note and read it. Ophelia had scrawled "What is up with you lately?" across the page. Kayley frowned and crumpled it back up, sticking it down in her bag.

What was up? Ophelia and Madeleine were

best friends. Madeleine was taking Kayley's spot in ballet and everywhere else. All Kayley had was her dancing, so it was time to harness that electricity she'd been feeling ever since stealing the shoes. Time to show them who was boss.

That mean feeling spiked again as she noticed Sophie and Emma whispering and looking over at them. She'd show them all at practice that night.

***

Madame made the same announcement at practice that all the teachers had.

"There *will* be searches tonight in your rooms. And anyone caught in possession of those shoes will be severely punished."

Kayley had to suppress a snort. Well, who in her right mind *would* keep the shoes? She was confident of her hiding place, but if she hadn't been, she would have hidden them in someone else's room. That way, they'd get in trouble.

Kayley shook herself. What a mean thought! She could be sarcastic and insensitive sometimes, but she was never deliberately cruel. She shook her head. Probably not enough sleep.

As Madame led the class through their warm-up, Kayley felt that electric feeling rush through her again.

And when it was time to dance, she knew she killed it. She bourréd off center with a genuine smile on her face, not the usual fake one she put on for performances. Madame looked her way with an approving glance.

Next, Madame clapped her hands and said, "OK, stepsisters. Sophie, Emma. Your part."

Kayley sat down and leaned into a wide stretch as Sophie and Emma took their places. Both started the first sequences for their parts in the show.

As they twirled, Kayley stared at them in a trance. She knew she was better than they were. That was why Madame had given her the part of fairy godmother in the first place. Madeleine, well, she was hard to compete with, though Kayley felt she had at least come close with her recent improvements. But Sophie and Emma weren't nearly as talented as Kayley.

Sophie hit an arabesque and then began her pirouette piqués. Kayley was concentrating so hard on Sophie's feet that her stare could have burned a hole in the floor.

And then Sophie's ankle turned.

The whole company seemed to gasp. Patrick stopped playing the piano with a string of wrong notes. Madame rushed to Sophie, crumpled on the ground. Emma held her hand.

"Patrick, be a dear and get the nurse, won't you?" Madame said.

Patrick nodded and rushed out of the room, coming back moments later with Nurse John. In one big movement, he picked up Sophie and carried her out.

The whole thing had happened so quickly that Kayley could barely breathe.

Madame came back in the room looking frazzled.

"Class dismissed for today."

The ballet dancers gathered their things quickly and walked out in twos and threes, talking excitedly. Emma took off to the nurse's station while Madeleine and Ophelia walked out together in their two-person huddle, barely noticing Kayley.

As she neared the door, Madame called out to her, "Kayley, you'll dance the part of the stepsister" and then hurriedly ran out the door, frazzled in a way Kayley had never seen her before.

It took a moment before the thought sunk in.

Kayley was no longer in the corps! She had a solo. Her heart leapt with joy.

But then she had a prickly little thought. What if she had somehow caused Sophie's accident? Maybe her good luck meant bad luck for others?

She shook her head. No. Sophie's accident was just that: an accident.

Heart lightened, Kayley practically skipped out the door, excited about ballet for the first time in a long while.

Chapter 10

At dinner, Kayley was so thrilled about her part, she hardly ate. But she was also bored of the dinner table conversation.

She sat at her normal place with Ophelia, Madeleine, and Emma, but it had been a few days since she had eaten with them and the whole situation felt weird. She stayed quiet, and she knew that was weird for everyone around her too. She picked at her vegetables.

Emma said, for the thousandth time,

"There was just no reason she should've turned her ankle. She's done those moves at so many practices . . . !"

Ophelia, who had ignored Emma the first 999 times, suddenly perked up. "Oh, there's a reason all right."

Emma and Madeleine leaned in while Kayley just crossed her arms over her chest. This ought to be good. Ophelia loved being in the spotlight and loved making stuff up. Normally, Kayley loved the stories Ophelia concocted, but she wasn't in the mood that night.

"It's because of the shoes, of course," Ophelia said. She picked up a green bean from her plate, ate it triumphantly, and sat back.

Now Kayley was interested. "What do you mean?" she asked. She hoped no one heard the hard edge in her voice. She cleared her throat and tried to soften her tone. "I mean, how could some old shoes in a case cause Sophie to turn her ankle?"

Ophelia smiled wide and leaned in again. "I heard they're a good luck charm for the school. As long as they stay public, you know, like, everyone's, they guard against bad things that happen to dancers. Now that they're gone, well . . ."

She shrugged, as if to say, who knew?

Emma's eyes grew wide. "This school is so weird, there are so many strange things that happen . . . I can totally see it."

That couldn't be true, Kayley thought. She shook off the idea and said, "Oh, come on. Sophie turned her ankle because ballet dancers get hurt! They just do! It happens."

Ophelia grabbed another green bean off her plate and said, "That's just the legend I heard. I remember hearing the maintenance man telling some freshman who asked why a pair of ratty shoes was in the case. He seemed to take the whole thing personally."

"Well, he must be going nuts, then, if that's the case," Madeleine said. "Someone stole those shoes right out from underneath him."

Emma shook her head. "I just don't get it. Who would do that? And how crazy . . . It must be someone who really needs some attention. I feel sorry for them."

Kayley dropped her fork. She bent under the table to pick it up, glad for the distraction. Emma felt sorry for her? Whatever. Who was the better dancer now? Maybe the company would be better off if Emma hurt herself too.

Once again, Kayley was startled by her own thought. Emma was her friend. And she had never wanted anyone to get hurt, ever. What was going on with her?

She put her fork on her plate and got up to leave, mumbling, "I'll see you guys tomorrow."

Emma stood up too. "I'll come with you. I want to go visit Sophie in her room. She is so bummed. Do you want to come with?"

Kayley swallowed guiltily. "Uh, I have a lot of homework to do since I missed yesterday."

Emma said, "Oh my gosh, I forgot you were sick. I was wondering why you'd been so quiet."

Kayley made her way to the dishes station, wishing Emma would just go visit Sophie and leave her alone.

Kayley gave an awkward laugh and said, "Yeah. I'm feeling better, though."

As Emma and Kayley started up the steps,

Kayley took a peek at Madeleine and Ophelia, still at the dinner table. They were looking up at Kayley, whispering once again. Suddenly, she was crazy nervous that they suspected something. She started walking faster up the stairs.

Emma kept pace with her. "Well, it sure seems like you're doing better, with your dancing, anyway. No offense, but things weren't looking that good for you for a while."

Kayley balled up her fists. How dare Emma say something like that? Who was she to judge Kayley's dancing?

And like that, Emma's feet came out from under her and she fell down the stairs.

Kayley looked at the bottom of the staircase and at Emma's twisted arm in shock. People thronged around Emma and began to help her up. What was going on?

And then a thought came, unbidden. Maybe Emma deserved that fall.

Kayley gasped at herself and felt the blood leave her face. Who was she turning into? She turned to run up the stairs, taking only one quick peek back at Emma and the throng of people.

She saw Ophelia eyeing her suspiciously.

Chapter 11

Back in her room, Kayley couldn't catch her breath.

She'd thought that Emma deserved to have an accident. And then she did.

She shook her head. But that was crazy to think she could *make* people have accidents. And anyway, the shoes were supposed to give Kayley *good* luck, not make other people have bad luck.

Unless maybe she couldn't have one without the other.

She took out her sushi slippers and peered in at the shoes. She took one out and stroked it.

It looked harmless enough. The shoe's design was just beautiful, and once again, Kayley felt mesmerized. She reached her hand into the second sushi slipper.

Then she jumped a mile high when a knock came at the door.

Quickly, she stuffed the one shoe back in her slipper as a voice carried through. It was the maintenance man.

"Room search. Open up."

Too paranoid to put the sushi slippers away, Kayley had an epiphany: she would wear the slippers with the shoes in them. She shoved her feet in the plush slippers, amazed that everything fit. She scooted along the floor and opened the door.

Madame stood with Bert and said, "A quick look through your room, Kayley. You may stay here while Bert searches."

Suddenly Kayley had a thought: he had seen her looking at the shoes. For the second time that night, her heart began to race.

She hoped she was as forgettable to him as he was to her.

He showed no signs of recognition as he began searching her room. She sat down on the bed and bounced her knee.

Madame stood by her. As Bert searched her shoes, Kayley felt ecstatic that she'd put the slippers on. Bert was practically tossing the rest of her footwear in the air—if he'd done that with her slippers, the pointe shoes would have surely flown out.

She looked down at her slippers and noticed the tip of a ribbon sticking out of the back of her slipper. When Madame spoke in her ear, she jumped yet again.

"I've been very impressed with your dancing as of late, Kayley. I see you took our talk to heart."

All Kayley could do was nod her head. She tried hard not to look down at her feet so that Madame wouldn't either.

Madame continued as Kayley started chewing on her fingernails. "All it took was a little extra effort on your part. It's good to see the fire back in your eyes."

She patted Kayley's shoulder, and Kayley shuddered so much that Madame drew her hand away as if she'd touched a hot stove.

Madame narrowed her eyes. "Are you OK, Kayley?"

Kayley nodded. "Yes, just tired."

Madame scrutinized her face. "Yes, you seem like it. You have dark circles under your eyes. When Bert's finished here, you should go right to bed."

Bert stood up. "I'm done here. No shoes here."

Kayley had a hard time not sighing with relief. She put one sushi slipper over the ribbon poking out and said, with real feeling, "Yes, I think I will go right to bed."

Madame nodded and walked out with Bert. "Remember, you have class tomorrow! And it seems as though everyone is getting hurt." She frowned, then turned back to Kayley. "Be careful tomorrow. We seem to be having a rash of bad luck."

When the door shut, Kayley dropped back in her bed. That was close. She was suddenly so tired she could barely keep her eyes open. But when she tried to sleep, nightmares of falling ballerinas kept her tossing and turning.

***

At morning class the next day, Kayley was almost an hour early. She'd gotten no sleep and although she could feel the weariness in her bones, the events of the past two days had made her so anxious that she welcomed the thought of dance practice.

After her warm-up, around five thirty, Ophelia stormed into the room.

"I thought I'd find you here." She crossed her arms across her chest. "What. Is. Going. On. With. You?"

Kayley stopped her turning. "What is going on with *you*?" she shot back, suddenly feeling the weeks of isolation. What had happened to the two of them?

"Me?" Ophelia said. "You're the one acting all strange! You stop trying at class, you don't care about anything . . . and then all of a sudden you stop talking to everyone and become this über-dancer!"

Kayley shot daggers with her eyes. "Jealous, much? And anyway, I'm surprised you even noticed, with your head so far up Madeleine's—"

"Yeah, right. I think *you're* the jealous one. Madeleine hasn't been acting like a freak. *You* were supposed to be my best friend, but you disappeared."

Kayley heard real disappointment in Ophelia's voice. A pang of longing shot through her. She did miss her best friend.

But then Ophelia's eyes hardened. "Anyway, like you could ever compare to me as a dancer."

Only Ophelia would say something like that. But instead of the rueful amusement Kayley normally would have felt, she felt rage.

She was twice the dancer Ophelia was now.

Madeleine walked in and seemed to see the sparks between Kayley and Ophelia.

"Guys?" she said timidly.

Kayley turned on her. "What."

Ophelia began to shout: "You are being such a b—"

Before Ophelia could finish, Madame walked in, along with most of the company. Practice commenced.

Kayley couldn't stop thinking about Ophelia's rude comments. When it was time for Ophelia's solo as Cinderella, Kayley stared at her with unrestrained hate.

Ophelia turned around and around in a quadruple pirouette, then performed a complicated series of movements that even Kayley couldn't take her eyes off of. But she kept thinking that maybe she could even be Cinderella if Ophelia were out of the picture. Then Kayley's parents would finally be proud of her. And Ophelia would get what she deserved.

As Kayley had the last thought, Ophelia landed a grand jeté. Her knee gave out beneath her and she collapsed to the floor.

The popping of the knee snapped Kayley out of her trance. This was the third time she'd had such vicious thoughts and the third time something happened about them.

Whatever else was going on, Kayley knew one thing: The shoes were causing bad luck all around her. Without asking to be excused, she ran to her room.

Chapter 12

Kayley sobbed on her bed. Everything was wrong.

All she wanted was to dance like she used to—instead, everyone she cared about was getting hurt. And she couldn't deny it anymore; she didn't like who she was becoming.

She had no friends anymore, she thought, and no peace of mind. Everything had gone wrong from the moment she had read about the shoes.

She didn't even care anymore if she had the fairy godmother part. All she wanted was for those she loved to be safe.

She decided to skip breakfast and classes and do some more research on the shoes. She tried to remember where she put the book she'd discovered in the back room of the library and finally found it under her bed.

Should she try to find another book that would help? Now that her friends had been hurt, Kayley didn't trust the first book at all. When she picked it up, it felt heavy. Even evil, if evil had a feeling. She could swear even her mood darkened. Why did she ever start reading the book in the first place?

She walked out of her room and headed straight into the library, back into the dusty old shelves, through the twist and turns that had led her to the dark corner once before.

Even during the day, the little space was completely creepy. The frail shaft of light that shined through the corner's one high window only exposed a solar system of dust particles.

She stuck the book on the first dusty shelf

she saw, shivering as she looked at the darkened space so hidden from the rest of the library. She couldn't even believe she had been back there once, and she sure wasn't going to do it again.

A voice startled her. "Can I help you?"

It was Geraldine, the librarian. Kayley had always liked Geraldine—about twenty years younger than most other teachers in the school, she always had some fun fashion thing going on. Today, her glasses sported skulls on the sides. She worked only part-time, so Kayley was surprised to see her on school grounds so early in the morning.

"Um . . . ," she stammered, hoping Geraldine hadn't seen her put the book back on the shelf.

"This area isn't for you," the librarian said. "No one, if you ask me, needs to ever go back here."

Kayley saw Geraldine shiver.

Then Kayley had an idea. "Is there a book about the legends of this building? Superstitions?"

Geraldine looked at her closely. "Are you wondering about the shoes?"

Kayley nodded and swallowed. "How did you know?" she asked, hoping she sounded nonchalant.

Geraldine chuckled. "It's a popular topic around here lately."

She squinted at Kayley. "I'll go ahead and tell you the current legend. But I hope you won't go spreading this nonsense around. I trust you to take it for the folderol it is."

Kayley didn't know what folderol was, but she was anxious to hear the legend. She nodded her head.

"OK." Geraldine's eyes twinkled. "Legend had it the shoes belonged to Headmaster Quincy's wife."

Kayley nodded impatiently. She knew this part.

"Well, the headmaster had terrible luck toward the end of his life. His wife was an amazing dancer, but she was killed onstage. Quincy was so taken with grief, he became convinced the shoes were to blame. To save the school—in his mind, anyway—he slept every night with the shoes by his bedside to make sure he alone would bear the bad luck. He nearly lost his fortune and everyone dear to him. Desperate, he took a glass case and locked the shoes inside.

"And legend has it, his luck turned around. He recovered his fortune and saved the school from closing. Supposedly, the case contained the bad luck of the shoes and kept them from infecting the grounds. In his will, the headmaster demanded that the shoes stay within the academy walls; the shoes can only be destroyed if the school is destroyed. The poor man was so delusional. He thought burning the shoes would send horrible luck out into the world. So Dario Quincy Academy keeps the shoes to this day! Or until a few days ago, anyway."

Kayley was taken aback. That wasn't the story she had read at all. But how had her dancing improved?

"How do you know all of this?" she asked.

Geraldine winked at her. "Well, when you get the academy's librarian job, you also become the keeper of its secrets." And then she walked away, leaving Kayley alone with her thoughts.

If what Geraldine said was true, she needed to get those shoes back in the case. And she would do it tonight.

She didn't care anymore if she danced well or not—it was time to do the right thing. It was time to take care of the people she loved instead of herself.

***

All throughout afternoon practice, Kayley was distracted. Madeleine had been promoted to the role of Cinderella, taking Ophelia's place. And Kayley was back in the fairy godmother spot.

It didn't feel good.

Although she danced well, her mind was elsewhere, thinking ahead to nighttime, when she could put the shoes back.

When it was Madeleine's turn to do her solo, Kayley's knees shook up and down. She started to chew on her fingernails.

As Madeleine did her piqué turns, Kayley noticed an antique light fixture swinging above the dance floor. And with horror, she saw a bolt pop out, then another.

Without thinking, she rushed away from the wall and pushed Madeleine out from underneath the fixture. The light crashed down in front of her. Madeleine lay on the floor, legs in split position, fallen but unhurt.

Madame Puant gasped. "Oh my word. Madeleine, Kayley, are you all right?"

They both nodded. The entire class began talking hysterically. Madame looked almost panicked, her eyes wild. "Class dismissed. No practice tomorrow. This place has become dangerous! Patrick, will you please call Bert?"

Kayley walked over to Madeleine and put her shaking hand on Madeleine's shoulder. "Are you OK?"

Madeleine, also shaking, nodded. "You saved my life," she said in wonder. Kayley felt tears behind her eyes.

"Can you come with me for a second?"

Madeleine's eyes got wide and she nodded.

Kayley pulled her into the hallway and waited until everyone was gone. Tears streamed down Kayley's face.

"It's my fault everyone is getting hurt."

Madeleine shook her head in bewilderment.

"Madeleine, I'm the one who took the shoes."

Chapter 13

Madeleine gasped. "Kayley!"

Kayley hiccup-sobbed. "I know!"

The whole story came tumbling out of her. She realized then how isolated she'd felt.

"I wanted to become a better dancer, and I read this book that said the shoes would make you a better dancer, but then I just found out that they don't make you a better dancer; they just give the school bad luck and people get hurt! . . . And it almost killed you, probably because I'm most jealous of how good a dancer you are and how you took Ophelia away."

Madeleine wrapped Kayley up in a hug.

"First," she said, her eyes boring into Kayley, "I didn't take Ophelia away. We've been talking a lot about why *you* have been so distant. She loves you, Kayley. You're her best friend. I can never take that away."

Kayley wiped her nose as another tear slid down her cheek.

"Second," Madeleine said, "You don't need any stupid shoes to make you a better dancer. You're a *wonderful* dancer. You just got lazy. Don't be mad at me for saying it, but you stopped coming to rehearsal early. You just stopped *caring*. The shoes had nothing to do with how you've danced lately. You just started putting some effort in!"

Kayley considered this for a moment. Maybe the electricity she felt wasn't about the shoes but about believing she could get to where she wanted to be.

"And third," Madeleine said. "We need to

get those shoes back into that case. When do you plan on doing it?"

"Are you saying you'll help me?"

Madeleine was at the academy on scholarship. If she were expelled, it was probably the end of her career. How could she offer something like that after Kayley had admitted to being so awful?

"You may not think so, Kayley, but people care about you. Including me. And as your friend, it's my duty to make sure I help you redeem yourself after something stupid."

Kayley sniffled and then grinned. "Well, you have your work cut out for you."

"I'll say. So, before we start planning, want one of these?" She pulled out a Twizzler, and Kayley's grin got bigger.

"Now we're talking."

***

"Man, this place is creepy," Madeleine whispered as she and Kayley sneaked into the lobby. At two in the morning, the red Exit light shone on the wall across from them. The glass shoe display stood empty and forlorn.

"You're telling me," Kayley whispered back.

What she didn't add was how much less creepy it was with a friend. For the eightieth time that day, she thanked her lucky stars for Madeleine. And the rest of her friends.

After Madeleine and Kayley had their talk, they had visited Ophelia's room and grabbed Sophie and Emma too. Kayley came clean and felt a kind of relief that she'd been missing for ages. Of course, Ophelia had called her a couple of choice words, but Kayley could swear she saw a softness in the girl's eyes. Kayley really did have the best friends ever.

Now, in the lobby, she had a chance to put everything to rest. She put the key in the case's keyhole and turned its handle.

And an alarm sounded throughout the school, a whooping, screeching, horrible alarm.

Chapter 14

Kayley turned to Madeleine with huge eyes and saw her friend mouth the word *run*.

So, Kayley ran. She ran so fast, she barely knew where she was running to. Until she realized she was running right toward the lobby staircase. A crowd had started to gather at the top.

Kayley skidded up to one of the stairway's outside curves and crouched down. She hoped-hoped-hoped no one would see her through the uprights of the banister. She hoped even harder that Madeleine had found a safe place.

Peeking between the banister's uprights, Kayley watched light flood the upper floor. Girls in pajamas stood whispering to one another. Madame Puant strode down the stairs with purpose and stopped in front of the glass case. Kayley backed up even farther against the wall, feeling exposed.

Just keep looking at the case, she prayed.

Bert stood by Madame Puant. Both of them looked disappointed.

Madame's eyes swept the room and, for a moment, Kayley saw Madame leaning over, Madame's back parallel with the slope of the stairs. But her eyes kept moving. Kayley breathed a sigh of relief.

Madame whispered something to Bert, then tapped her cane against the floor.

"To bed everyone! Nothing to see here."

With the maintenance man behind her, she began her climb back up the staircase.

Kayley briefly saw Ophelia, Sophie, and Emma looking around at the top of the stairs.

She knew they were worried about her and Madeleine. Finally, they also returned to their rooms, and the lights went out again.

Kayley's heartbeat slowed to a normal pace. She could only hope that Madeleine had joined the rest of the group and gone up to bed.

Since the case was already unlocked, Kayley told herself she still had a shot. Run over. Toss the shoes inside. Get away.

She tiptoed over to the case and opened it with care, cringing at the possibility that her touch would set the alarm off again. Setting the shoes back on display, she felt a gigantic weight lift off her shoulders.

Then she jumped about five feet in the air. Without a sound, Madeleine had appeared at her side. She grabbed Kayley's sleeve and said, "Let's go! That was way too close for comfort."

Not waiting for a reply, Madeline moved toward the stairs.

"Where are you going?" Kayley said.

"To my room. I want to get out of here!"

Kayley sighed. "Well, we're not quite done. We have to get this key back to the maintenance man's room."

Chapter 15

Madeleine closed her eyes and whispered, "Are you serious?"

Kayley nodded. "Yes, but you don't have to come!"

"Didn't we resolve that earlier?" Madeline replied. "We're in this together."

The warm feeling Kayley felt earlier flooded back. Yeah. Friends were pretty awesome.

"The stairway to his office is near the nurse's station," Kayley said. "If you keep watch at the top of the stairs, I can run down and put the key back where I found it."

Madeleine nodded, but Kayley could see her face was pale. Time to get this over with.

They tiptoed to the nurse's station, and Kayley peered down the dark stairs. No TV light came from Bert's room this time. Kayley's stomach tied itself in a knot.

Madeleine seemed to sense her unease. "Should I head down with you?"

Kayley shook her head. As much as she wanted Madeline by her side, it was time for her to take responsibility. She started down the lower stairway, aware of every creak.

When she got to the bottom of the stairs, she hesitated. Bert's office was pitch-black except for the bead of red light from his DVD/VCR player. She squared her shoulders and walked in.

In about a minute's time, her eyes adjusted and she could make out the outlines of shelves, a desk, a chair. She made her way over to Bert's desk, ducked down, and tapped her hand along the wall.

She couldn't feel the little door.

Frantically, she ran her hands all around the wall, squinting to see if she could make out the tiny cabinet door.

There was nothing there.

Then she heard footsteps coming down the hall—and whistling.

Bert was back. Kayley hid in the space under the desk, closing her eyes tightly. It was just a matter of minutes before he caught her.

A light came on in the office, and Kayley shut her eyes tighter. She waited to hear Bert's voice, yelling at her.

Instead, she heard a *whooooooooo-oooo*, traveling like a strange wind through the office door. Kayley peeked under the desk and saw Bert's feet pointed toward the door.

In a shaking voice, Bert said, "Who's there?"

The *whooooooooo-oooo* came again. This time Kayley recognized the voice: Madeleine. Her eyes teared up—Madeleine was saving Kayley's skin. And risking her own.

Bert grabbed something off the desk and said, "Quincy house, you won't get the best of me!"

His feet disappeared, and Kayley soon heard

him running up the stairs. She wished with all her heart that Madeleine had hidden well again.

She turned back to the wall and spotted, in the light, the little outline marking the key's rightful home. As she crouched down to open the door, Kayley heard something else. The sound started like a whisper and seemed to come along a breeze toward her. A laugh, cold and evil.

Kayley dropped the key on the floor and dashed out of the room. The climb up the stairs to the nurse's station felt like the longest she'd ever taken. Even the chance of Bert being there didn't slow her down. As she reached the top, a hand crawled around the corner and grabbed her.

Kayley squealed.

"It's me," Madeleine whispered. "Just me!"

Kayley stepped back, her hand on her heart.

"I barely ducked out of the way of Bert. He tore down the hall in the other direction." Madeleine gave a little smile. "I know why *he* was freaked out, but what got into you? You know that *whoo* sound was me, right?"

Kayley shook her head. "No time. Must go now."

She grabbed Madeleine's hand and took off down the hallway, occasionally checking back to see that no monsters had followed them.

***

Kayley ended up sleeping in Ophelia's room, as did Madeleine, Sophie, and Emma. Kayley was way too freaked to be alone, and because it was Friday, academy rules said the students could have sleepovers. When Madeleine and Kayley had arrived at Ophelia's, they collapsed and said they'd answer questions in the morning. At breakfast the five girls huddled around the table together.

Madame Puant came into the dining hall just as breakfast started. "I want you to all know that the shoes have been located and are safely back in their case."

Murmurs broke out among all the students. Sophie, Emma, Ophelia, Madeleine, and Kayley all gave each other knowing looks.

Madame went on. "Because of recent

injuries, we are canceling the production of *Cinderella*, but we'll begin to prepare for *The Nutcracker* across the next few weeks." Kayley could swear Madame looked directly at her. "Make sure you continue to practice and keep in shape until then."

Madame swept out of the dining hall, and the normal chatter took over the room once again.

Ophelia leaned over the dining table. "So, you put the ... uh, things ... back. But what happened with the key?"

Kayley could feel her face lose color. "First, Madeleine saved my butt. Bert almost caught me. Second, I know I'm going to sound crazy. And you know me. I don't believe in this stuff. But when I was trying to put the key back? I heard this laugh. This super-evil laugh."

The girls looked at each other. Not one of them laughed.

Ophelia sat back in her chair. "There is something very wrong at Dario Quincy Academy," she said gravely. "We've all felt it. And I think it tried to hurt all of us. No matter what happens, no matter who gets what part, or whatever, we all need to stick together. Deal?"

Ophelia met eyes with everyone. They all nodded their heads and joined hands in the middle of the table.

Kayley didn't even care how weird it must have looked to the other students at breakfast. They had one another and that was all that mattered.

Epilogue

Madame handed the man a mint—her fanciest kind—and sat behind her desk with a smile.

"I'm sorry to be rude, Mr. Johnson, and don't think me unappreciative of your time, but why is it you've come again?"

Mr. Johnson examined the mint and frowned. "Madame Puant. Betsy. I think you know exactly why I'm here."

Madame sighed, her shoulders slumping. "Yes. Yes, I do."

"My great-great-great grandfather did everything in his power to protect this school. But sometimes that's just not enough. Now, because of my love for my family, I am loath to get rid of this place. Nor am I excited about what might happen to myself and my family if I do . . . but I'll be damned if I let the children here get hurt."

"Sir, I would never allow harm to befall my students. How dare you suggest such a thing!"

He waved his hand. "What I'm *suggesting* is that if we can't get things under control here, if we can't contain the . . . uh, misfortune . . . Well, I'm afraid I'll have no choice but to demolish this place."

Madame slumped again. "I understand. But these children . . . are exceptional. And we nurture them and this dance . . ."

Mr. Johnson nodded. "Even so, you must agree: This house makes people do strange things. Strange even to them. Did you punish the girl?"

Madame shook her head. "No. The circumstances were punishment enough. And

I knew she would choose correctly eventually."

Mr. Johnson nodded and stood up. "Well, then. We are in agreement. We need to put a stronger lid on the more eccentric qualities of this place. And if that can't happen, then I'm afraid the Quincy Academy will be no more."

THE DARIO QUINCY ACADEMY OF DANCE

Ballet. Gossip. Evil Spirits.

SEEK THE TRUTH

AND FIND THE CAUSE

WITH

THE PARANORMALISTS

THE HAUNTING OF
APARTMENT 101

MEGAN ATWOOD

THE TERROR OF
BLACK EAGLE TAVERN

MEGAN ATWOOD

THE MAYHEM ON
MOHAWK AVENUE

MEGAN ATWOOD

THE BRIDGE OF
DEATH

MEGAN ATWOOD

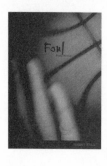

About the Author

Megan Atwood is the author of more than fourteen books for children and young adults and is a college teacher who teaches all kinds of writing. She clearly has the best job in the world. She lives in Minneapolis, Minnesota, with two cats, a boy, and probably a couple of ghosts.